P9-DWI-087

The Boxcar Children
Surprise Island
The Yellow House Mystery
Mystery Ranch
Mike's Mystery
Blue Bay Mystery
The Woodshed Mystery
The Lighthouse Mystery
Mountain Top Mystery
Schoolhouse Mystery
Caboose Mystery
Houseboat Mystery
Snowbound Mystery
Tree House Mystery
Bicycle Mystery
Mystery in the Sand
Mystery Behind the Wall
Bus Station Mystery
Benny Uncovers a Mystery
The Haunted Cabin Mystery
The Deserted Library Mystery
The Animal Shelter Mystery
The Old Motel Mystery
The Mystery of the Hidden Painting
The Amusement Park Mystery
The Mystery of the Mixed-Up Zoo
The Camp-Out Mystery
The Mystery Girl
The Mystery Cruise
The Disappearing Friend Mystery
The Mystery of the Singing Ghost
The Mystery in the Snow
The Pizza Mystery
The Mystery Horse
The Mystery at the Dog Show
The Castle Mystery
The Mystery of the Lost Village
The Mystery on the Ice
The Mystery of the Purple Pool
The Ghost Ship Mystery
The Mystery in Washington, DC
The Canoe Trip Mystery

The Mystery of the Hidden Beach
The Mystery of the Missing Cat
The Mystery at Snowflake Inn
The Mystery on Stage
The Dinosaur Mystery
The Mystery of the Stolen Music
The Mystery at the Ball Park
The Chocolate Sundae Mystery
The Mystery of the Hot Air Balloon
The Mystery Bookstore
The Pilgrim Village Mystery
The Mystery of the Stolen Boxcar
The Mystery in the Cave
The Mystery on the Train
The Mystery at the Fair
The Mystery of the Lost Mine
The Guide Dog Mystery
The Hurricane Mystery
The Pet Shop Mystery
The Mystery of the Secret Message
The Firehouse Mystery
The Mystery in San Francisco
The Niagara Falls Mystery
The Mystery at the Alamo
The Outer Space Mystery
The Soccer Mystery
The Mystery in the Old Attic
The Growling Bear Mystery
The Mystery of the Lake Monster
The Mystery at Peacock Hall
The Windy City Mystery
The Black Pearl Mystery
The Cereal Box Mystery
The Panther Mystery
The Mystery of the Queen's Jewels
The Stolen Sword Mystery
The Basketball Mystery
The Movie Star Mystery
The Mystery of the Pirate's Map
The Ghost Town Mystery
The Mystery of the Black Raven
The Mystery in the Mall

THE GAME STORE MYSTERY

created by
GERTRUDE CHANDLER WARNER

Illustrated by Robert Papp

Albert Whitman & Company
Chicago, Illinois

Printed in the United States of America
10 9 8 7 6 5 LB 22 21 20 19 18 17

Illustrated by Robert Papp

Visit the Boxcar Children online at www.boxcarchildren.com.
For more information about Albert Whitman & Company,
visit our website at www.albertwhitman.com.

Contents

THE GAME STORE MYSTERY

CHAPTER 1

Missing Letters

"O_ _N_NG . . . _O_DAY," six-year-old Benny Alden struggled to sound out the words on the sign in front of the newly built Crossroads Mall. "TH_ . . . G_M_ . . . S_ _T . . . ?" He scratched his head as Grandfather steered the van into the mall parking lot. "I don't get it."

"I think there are some letters missing on that sign, Benny." Twelve-year-old Jessie smiled at her younger brother. "That's why the words don't make sense."

"Oh." Benny was already a pretty good

reader, but he was trying to get even better. "What would the sign say if all the letters were there?"

Grandfather pulled into a parking spot right in front of the sign. Deep red roses bloomed all around it.

The children puzzled out the message a little longer. Finally, ten-year-old Violet spoke up. "I think it's supposed to say 'Opening Today. The Game Spot.'"

"Of course!" Fourteen-year-old Henry slapped his hand to his forehead. "Good job, Violet."

The Game Spot was Queenie Polk's store. Queenie was an old friend of their grandfather's, and she had invited the Aldens to come down and see her new store today.

"I don't know, kids," Grandfather said as everyone hopped out of the van. "TH_ . . . G_M_ . . . S_ _T . . . must be the Game Spot. Those letters don't fit the names of the other stores here. But I don't think the Game Spot is opening yet today. Queenie said she had several last-minute details to take care of before she could open."

"And look. There's a space after the O and before 'day,'" Jessie pointed out. "That means there's another letter after the O in that word."

"So what else could the word be?" Benny asked.

Violet walked closer to the sign. "Let's see . . . there's an O in *Monday*. It could be *Monday*."

"Is there an O in *Tuesday*?" Benny asked.

"No," Henry replied. "And there isn't one in *Wednesday, Thursday, Friday, Saturday* or *Sunday*, either."

"Then I bet the sign is supposed to say: THE GAME SPOT. OPENING MON-DAY!" Violet said triumphantly.

Grandfather smiled at them. "You children are good detectives."

"Yes, we are," Jessie agreed, thinking of all the mysteries she and her brothers and sister had solved. "But we're also good at word games. Figuring out what this sign was supposed to say is really just a word game."

"That's true," Grandfather said. "Queenie

likes word games, too. You'll have to see if she's got any new games to recommend to you. Shall we go say hello to her?"

"Oh, yes," the children said.

The Game Spot was located right in the middle of the mall, between Lake's Jewelry Store and an empty storefront. There was a drugstore at one end of the mall, a coffee shop at the other, and several empty storefronts in between.

The door to the Game Spot was propped open with a folding chair that had a "Help Wanted" sign hanging from it. A man dressed in old jeans and a faded shirt was carefully etching the store hours into the glass window. The Aldens walked past him and went inside.

A radio played country music in the background. Several people bustled around stacking merchandise on shelves. The whole place smelled like fresh paint.

"Hey, look at this!" Benny made a beeline for a model train that was set up in the window. "Doesn't the third car look like our boxcar?"

"It does, Benny," Violet said.

The children had actually lived in a box-car for a short time after their parents died. They didn't know their grandfather then. They were afraid he'd be mean. So instead of going to live with him, they ran away. They found an old boxcar in the woods and made it their home. But when Grandfather found them, they saw he wasn't mean at all. He even moved the boxcar to their backyard so the children could still play in it.

"James Alden? Is that you?" A middle-aged woman who was no taller than Violet came down the aisle toward them. Her copper-colored hair was twisted into a bun and fastened at the nape of her neck. She had a big smile on her face.

"Queenie!" Grandfather moved toward the woman with his hand outstretched. "How are you?"

"Just fine," Queenie replied as the grown-ups shook hands. "These must be your lovely grandchildren."

"Yes. This is Henry, Jessie, Violet, and

Benny." Grandfather introduced them each in turn.

The children said hello and shook hands with Queenie.

"I'm happy to meet you all. What do you think of my new store?" She stepped back so the Aldens could take a good look around.

"It looks great," Henry said, gazing at the wide aisles stocked with games, puzzles and hobby supplies. Off to the side was a small sitting area with tables and chairs. "It looks like you're almost ready to open."

"Almost," Queenie agreed. She looked both excited and nervous at the same time. "Most of the inventory is out on the shelves. I'm still hoping to hire another employee or two. And of course, the building inspector still needs to come. But I should be able to open on Monday."

"That's what we thought," Benny said. He told Queenie about the sign out front with the missing letters and how he and the others had figured out what the sign was supposed to say.

"Yes, I noticed that sign when I came in this morning," Queenie said. "I already talked to George about it. He's the person who owns this mall. He said he'd be out later today with some spare letters to fix that sign."

"That's good," Grandfather said.

"Hmph," said a voice behind them.

The Aldens turned to see a man around Queenie's age stocking shelves. He was tall and thin with dark hair that was graying at the temples.

"I wouldn't count on George coming out today, Queenie," the man said as he shifted some boxes on the shelf to make room for the boxes on the floor.

"He said he would," Queenie said.

"That's what he said the day you had trouble with those new pipes," the man replied.

"Oh, Carter. Don't be unpleasant. I'm sure George will come when he can. In the meantime, why don't you say hello to the Aldens. James, this is my good friend, Carter Malone. He lends me a hand sometimes."

"Pleased to meet you, Carter," Grandfather said.

"You, too," Carter said as he stooped to pick up the boxes on the floor.

"Hey, what's that game you've got there?" Jessie craned her neck to see the box top. "It looks like a word game."

"It is," Queenie replied. "It's called Word Master. You start out by looking at a list of letters. Then there are two things you're trying to do. One, you want to see how many words you can find in that list of letters. And two, you're trying to fit the words together into a message. It's a great game, and Carter here is a true 'Word Master.'"

"Really?" Jessie said. "Could you show me how to play, Carter?"

"Oh, I don't know." Carter looked a little uncomfortable.

"Well, I know you're busy," Jessie said. "It doesn't have to be right now."

"Nonsense," Queenie waved her hand. "Carter, you could use a break. Why don't you take the Aldens into the back room and show them how to play."

Carter blushed. "I don't think so," he said, refusing to meet the children's eyes. Then he hurried away without giving any further explanation.

Queenie frowned at his back. "You'll have to excuse Carter," she said as she grabbed a Word Master box off the shelf and handed it to Jessie. "He's shy, and he doesn't spend much time with children. He loves games, though. And he's helped me so much with this store. He gets insulted if I try to pay him. Believe me, beneath that gruff exterior beats a heart of gold."

"Any friend of yours, Queenie, is a friend of ours," Grandfather said.

Queenie glanced toward the back of the store. "Just let me check on the man who's installing my safe, and then we'll set up a game, okay?"

The Aldens followed Queenie to the back of the store. A man with a dark mustache was just coming out of the back room. There was a patch on his shirt that said SILVER SAFES.

"Oh. Are you finished, Tony?" Queenie asked the man.

"Yes." Tony set his toolbox on the floor and handed Queenie a clipboard. "Would you sign, please?"

Queenie signed her name, then gave the clipboard back to Tony.

Tony handed Queenie a small booklet and a separate piece of paper. "Here's your owner's manual and your combination. Give me a call if you have any trouble."

"I will," Queenie said. "Thanks, Tony."

As Tony bent down to pick up his toolbox, he noticed the game in Jessie's hands. "Word Master, huh? That's my favorite game."

"Is it?" Queenie smiled. "Well, then you'll have to stop back for a game sometime. That's why I set up that sitting area in the front of the store. I'm hoping my store will become a place where people will hang out and play games."

"That sounds fun. I'll try and stop in sometime next week," Tony said. He shook hands with Queenie, then left.

"You mean people can come in here anytime and play games with other people who are in the store?" Violet asked.

"Yes," Queenie replied. "I never just wanted a store where people just come in, buy things, then leave. I want people to stay and make friends."

"Even kids?" Benny asked.

"Especially kids!" Queenie gave Benny's shoulders a squeeze. "In fact, I'd also like to arrange an area just for kids here in the store. I'm planning to call it the Kids' Korner. I was hoping you children would help me design it?"

"Really?" Violet asked.

"Absolutely," Queenie said. "That's why I asked your grandfather to bring you in here today. Perhaps we can talk about some ideas after we play a quick game of Word Master."

The Aldens all nodded enthusiastically as they moved closer to the back room. But before they got there, they heard sirens.

The noise grew louder and louder until it sounded like it was right outside the store!

"What's going on?" Henry asked. They all exchanged worried looks.

"I don't know," Queenie said. "Let's go find out."

CHAPTER 2

Robbed!

There were two police cars parked in front of the coffee shop at the end of the mall. A small crowd had gathered in front of the shop. The Aldens pressed closer to see what was going on.

"Do you know why the police are here?" Jessie asked a woman in a red jacket who stood at the edge of the crowd.

The woman turned. "Didn't you hear? The Java Café was robbed last night!"

"Robbed!" Henry exclaimed.

"Oh, no," Queenie said, pressing her hand to her mouth.

Carter Malone stepped closer to Queenie. "What happened?" he asked the woman in red.

"I don't know the specifics," she replied. "All I know is that woman over there," she pointed to a very distraught-looking young woman with straight blond hair, "came in to work this morning and found the safe standing wide open. Everything inside it was gone."

"Oh, my goodness," Queenie said. "That's Raina Holt. I know her! I play bridge with her mother."

"Are you the owner of this establishment?" a female police officer asked the brown-haired man who was standing next to Raina.

Benny had to stand on his tiptoes in order to see.

"Yes. I'm Chip Douglas. I just opened up about three weeks ago." Chip wore a long, white apron over jeans and a blue shirt. His hair hung almost to his shoulders.

"Do you have any idea what happened?" a male officer asked.

Chip's eyes narrowed. "I have a pretty good idea. Let me introduce you to my assistant manager . . . or should I say *former* assistant manager, Raina Holt."

Raina gasped. "No! You can't fire me, Chip. Please! I need this job!"

"You should have thought of that before you stole from me," Chip countered.

"How does he know that she's stolen from him?" Violet whispered to Queenie, who was standing beside her.

"I don't know," Queenie whispered back. "But I have a hard time believing she did."

"I didn't steal anything," Raina insisted.

"Excuse me," a round man with a balding head said as he made his way through the crowd. "Let me through, please. I'm George Berber. I own this mall. Would somebody please tell me what happened?" George asked as he glanced from one police officer to the other.

The female officer introduced herself to George. "I'm Detective Owen. And this is my partner, Detective Bryant." She gestured toward the other detective, who nodded at George.

"Ms. Holt here is an employee at the Java Café," Detective Owen went on. "She came in this morning and discovered someone had broken into the safe in the back room. Is that right, Ms. Holt?"

"Yes." Raina nodded.

"Listen, she's the one who locked up last night, and she's the one who opened up this morning," Chip told the officers. "There's no sign of forced entry. Nothing out of place. And she's the only one besides me who knows the combination to the safe—"

"Please, Mr. Douglas," Detective Owen rested a hand on his shoulder. "I'd like to hear from Raina first. She's the one who was here. I promise we'll hear from you, too."

Everyone turned to Raina. She looked like a frightened animal.

"I—I don't know what to say," Raina said, stepping back.

"Just tell us what happened, ma'am,"

Detective Bryant said. He held a pencil and small pad of paper in his hands.

"Well, I closed up last night—" Raina began.

"Was there anybody else in the shop when you closed up?" Detective Bryant interrupted.

"No." Raina shook her head. "It was just me. The last customer left about ten minutes before closing. I locked the front door first, then the back door. Then I counted out the money in the drawer and put it in the safe for Chip like I always do. After that, I went out the back door and drove home. That's it."

"Are you sure the door was locked when you left?" Detective Bryant asked.

"Yes," Raina replied. "I always double-check once I'm outside. The door was locked. I'm sure of it. And it was still locked when I came in this morning."

Chip let out a heavy sigh. It was clear he didn't believe a word Raina was saying.

"So what happened when you arrived this morning?" Detective Owen asked.

"Well, I came in around nine o'clock," Raina explained. "I went in through the back door and found the empty safe standing wide open. I called 911 first. Then I called Chip."

Chip couldn't hold back any longer. "I'm telling you, she's the thief!" He pointed at Raina.

Queenie pushed her way through the crowd until she was standing next to Raina. "I've known Raina Holt since she was a little girl. She isn't a thief!"

Raina sniffed. "Thank you, Queenie," she said gratefully.

Chip snorted. "If that's what you think, then you've got your head in the sand," he said.

"I'm sorry, sir." Detective Bryant closed up his notebook. "We don't have enough evidence to arrest this young lady. But if you don't mind, we'd like to look around a little inside the store and see what else we might find."

Chip nodded. "Go ahead," he told the two officers as he held the door open.

"I better come, too," George Berber said as he followed the officers into the shop. "I'm not very happy to hear there's been a robbery in my mall."

Raina moved toward the shop, too, but Chip blocked her path. "I just want you to get your stuff out of the back room and leave," he told her. "You're fired!"

Raina's eyes filled with tears.

Chip turned his back to Raina. He stood in the doorway watching the officers work inside the shop.

Raina buried her face in her hands and started to cry.

Queenie went to her and pulled the girl into her arms. "Shh," Queenie said, stroking the girl's hair. "It's okay."

"But I didn't steal anything," Raina cried.

"I know you didn't, honey," Queenie said.

"And I needed that job," Raina sobbed. "I've got an apartment to pay for. And college tuition. What am I going to do without a job?"

"I tell you what," Queenie said as the crowd started to disperse. "I still need to hire another cashier for the Game Spot. Are you interested?"

Raina blinked a few times. "Y-you'd hire me?" she said, wiping the back of her hand across her eyes. "Even after you heard what Chip said about me?"

"Of course I would," Queenie said. "This is crazy. You don't want to work for somebody who doesn't trust you, do you, Raina?"

"No," Raina sniffled.

"I pay two dollars above minimum wage, and I pay the first and third Fridays of the month. Will that work for you?"

Raina nodded. She dried her eyes again.

"Then why don't you go and get your things from the Java Café. These are my friends Jessie and Henry Alden. They'll go with you. Then come on back to the Game Spot, and we'll get started."

"Okay. Thank you, Queenie," Raina said appreciatively.

So Jessie and Henry walked Raina back to the Java Café while Grandfather, Violet and Benny went back to the Game Spot with Queenie and Carter.

Chip stopped Jessie and Henry at the door. "You kids can wait here," he said. "I don't want you getting in the officers' way."

Neither Jessie nor Henry had any intention of getting in anyone's way, but they didn't want to upset Chip any further, either, so they stayed outside. But through the window they could see Chip following Raina all the way to the back room.

"I feel bad for Raina," Jessie said. "She doesn't seem like the type of person who would steal from her boss."

"We don't know her very well," Henry said. "But I agree with you, Jessie. She's clearly very upset about everything that's happened."

While Jessie and Henry waited in front of the Java Café, an older man with a binder full of plastic letters in his hand walked up to them.

"Hello, there," he said to Jessie and Henry. "I'm George Berber, the mall owner. I understand you're friends of Queenie's."

"That's right," Henry said.

"How would you like to help me put these letters up on that sign over there?" George asked.

"Sure," Jessie said. She and Henry followed George across the parking lot.

"Be careful of the roses," George said. "You wouldn't want to get scratched."

"Are the police finding any clues?" Henry asked as he and Jessie carefully picked their way over to the sign.

"I'm afraid not." George shook his head. "It's like Chip said. Nothing's out of place. Nothing else has been touched. It looks like whoever broke in had a key."

"How many people had a key to the Java Café?" Jessie wanted to know.

"Not many," George replied. "Just Chip and Raina. And of course, me. I have a key to all the stores here. I hope your friend Queenie knows what she's doing hiring that girl. I'm not sure *I'd* hire her."

George opened his binder and took out some letters. He handed some to Henry and some to Jessie. "All you have to do is slide them into place like this," he explained as he replaced the missing P, E, and I in the word OPENING.

Jessie added the M and N to the word MONDAY and the P and O to the word SPOT. And Henry added the E to the word THE and the A and E to the word GAME.

"There," Henry said, stepping back to admire their work. "It's all fixed."

Raina came out of the Java Café with her jacket and purse slung over one arm. Her cheeks were streaked with tears. Before the door closed behind her, Chip ran out. "Hey! How about my key?" he called after her.

Raina stopped. She opened her purse, pulled out a single key on a chain, and slammed it into Chip's hand.

* * * *

"It's too bad about the robbery at the Java Café," Henry said that night when the Aldens all sat down to dinner.

"I hope the police catch the person who did it," Violet said as she helped herself to a piece of fried chicken, then passed the platter to Jessie.

"I'm sure they will, Violet," said Grandfather.

"And I hope Raina really is innocent," Benny said.

"Queenie thinks she is," Jessie said. "That was nice of her to hire Raina on the spot like that."

"It was also nice of her to ask us to help her set up a Kids' Korner in the store," Violet said. "That's going to be fun."

"Yes, it is," said Jessie and Henry.

Benny remained silent as he rolled his peas around on his plate.

"Don't you think that'll be fun, Benny?" Jessie asked.

Benny shrugged. "It sounds fun. I just wish that Queenie's store was in a different mall."

"Why?" Violet asked. "The Crossroads Mall is brand new. It's a great place for a game store."

"Yeah, but there's already been a lot of trouble there," Benny explained. "First the letters on the sign out front were all mixed up. Then somebody broke into the safe at the coffee shop. What's going to happen next?"

"I don't think anything else will happen," Grandfather said. "The mall owner already replaced the missing letters. And the police are looking into the robbery. Everything is going to be fine there now."

"But if it isn't," said Benny, "then maybe we'll have another mystery to solve."

CHAPTER 3

The Lost Key

The Aldens had been brainstorming ideas for the Game Spot's Kids' Korner all weekend. Queenie had asked them to come back on Monday afternoon with a list of possibilities. So after lunch they got on their bikes and rode over to the Crossroads Mall.

"GR . . . grand OPENING TODAY," Benny read the new message on the sign in the mall parking lot. "THE GAME SPOT."

"I'm glad all the letters are there today,"

Violet said as they locked their bikes to the
bike rack under a tall maple tree.

"So am I," Henry said.

The children walked into the store and
were happy to see that Queenie had customers already on her first day. Raina was
at the cash register ringing up two puzzles
for a little girl and her mother.

Raina looked a lot more cheerful today
than the last time the Aldens had seen her.
Her long blond hair was tied back neatly
with a ribbon. She smiled and waved at the
children, then turned back to her customer.

"That's fifteen fifty-five," Raina said.

The mother handed her a twenty.

"Four forty-five is your change." Raina
handed the mother some bills and coins.
"Thank you." Once they were gone, Raina
turned to the Aldens. "It's good to see you
kids again. Queenie is over in the puzzles.
I know she's anxious to talk to you."

"Thanks," Henry said. "We'll go find
her."

The children headed over to the puzzles
Queenie and her friend Carter were talking

at the opposite end of the aisle.

"We can move this shelf over here," Queenie said. "Then we should have room."

"Yes, but the aisle will still feel crowded. I don't understand why you want this 'Kids' Korner.' This isn't a toy store."

"No, it's a game store," Queenie explained. "Children play games too, Carter. And I want children to feel just as welcome here as adults do."

"Whatever you say, Queenie," Carter said with a sigh.

Queenie turned then and noticed the Aldens. "Oh, hello!" she said with a big smile. "I was hoping you kids would get here soon."

But Carter didn't look as happy to see them as Queenie did.

"I'm thinking of moving this shelf," Queenie told the Aldens. "Then we can put the Kids' Korner over there." She pointed to the back corner of the store. Do you think that's a big enough area?"

"I think so," Henry said. The others nodded.

Carter sighed. "I guess I'll start moving the merchandise off the shelf so it can be moved."

"Thank you, Carter," Queenie said. "I appreciate that." Then she turned back to the Aldens. "Have you come up with any ideas to make the area look inviting?"

"Well," Jessie began. "We were thinking you should start with some brightly colored tables and chairs. Something in red, yellow, blue, or green."

"Maybe even all four colors," Benny put in.

"That would be nice!" said Queenie.

"If you can't find tables and chairs in bright colors, you could just get whatever you want and we'll paint them for you," Henry offered.

"I think you should have some big, fluffy pillows for kids who want to sit on the floor and put puzzles together," Benny said.

"Those are both very good ideas," Queenie said thoughtfully. She strolled slowly around the area as though trying to imagine it. "What about the walls?"

"We could paint a mural or something on this wall over here," Violet suggested. "Maybe we could paint a row of children from different countries all holding hands or something?"

"Could you?" Queenie asked.

"Violet's a wonderful artist, Queenie," Jessie said as Violet blushed.

"Yes, she is," Henry agreed. "She could draw it all out in pencil first and then we could all help her paint it."

"How soon do you think you could get started?" Queenie asked.

"I could start sketching right now, if you'd like," Violet said.

"I'd like that very much," Queenie said. "Let's go see if we can find you a pencil." She headed to the front of the store. The Aldens followed.

Tony Silver, the man who had installed Queenie's safe last week, fell into step behind them. He had a Word Master game in his hands.

"Hello, Tony," Queenie said, smiling at him. "How are you?"

"Just fine," he replied as he set his box on the counter so he could pay for it. "I decided I needed a new copy of this game. My set is missing a few letters."

Queenie walked back behind the counter. "It's hard to play Word Master if you're missing some letters," she said.

"Yes, it is," Tony agreed. He reached into his back pocket and pulled out his billfold. "Say, I was wondering, Queenie. Have you thought about hosting a Word Master tournament in here?"

"Actually, I have," Queenie said as she took Tony's money. "Carter suggested it just a few days ago. He thought it would be a good way to get people into the store."

"All you have to do is pick a date and put up some flyers," Carter said.

Queenie thought for a minute. "How about two weeks from Saturday, starting at noon? We could have two divisions. One for adults and another for children."

"That sounds good," Carter said. The others nodded.

"We could help with the flyers," Jessie

said. "We could make them and distribute them."

"That's a wonderful idea," Queenie said. She bent down and grabbed some paper and pencils from the shelf below the cash register. "Perhaps while Violet is sketching ideas for the mural, the rest of you can work on flyers?"

"We'd be happy to," Henry replied.

"So, how's that safe working out for you?" Tony asked. "Are you happy with it?"

"Oh, yes," Queenie said. "It seems very secure. The only problem is I don't like the combination. It's hard to remember. Is it possible to change it?"

"Sure. I'd be happy to show you," Tony said.

Tony and Queenie went to the back room. Violet took a pencil over to the wall. And Henry, Jessie, and Benny took their paper and pencils over to a table to work on the flyer.

Jessie started lettering the words WORD MASTER TOURNAMENT at the top.

"We should draw some people having fun

playing Word Master, too," Benny said.

"Good idea, Benny. Would you like to draw them?" Jessie slid the paper over to him so he could draw.

A few minutes later, Queenie and Tony came out of the back room. They stopped up by the cash register and Queenie lay a scrap of paper on the counter.

Carter was back behind the counter with Raina. He glanced at the paper Queenie had just set down.

"Is this the new combination to your safe?" Carter asked.

"Yes," Queenie replied. "QUEEN. That should be easy to remember, don't you think? At least it's a word rather than just a series of letters."

Carter grabbed the paper and tore it into little pieces. "Careful, Queenie. You don't want to leave the combination to your safe lying around. And you certainly don't say what the combination is out loud!"

"Oh, Carter. Don't worry so much." Queenie laughed. "There's nobody in here."

Carter glanced suspiciously at the Aldens.

"There are kids in here," he said in a low voice. But it wasn't so low that the children couldn't hear.

"We're not going to break into any safes," Benny said.

"Of course we're not," Jessie said to him. "But still, Carter has a point. If you have a safe, you shouldn't say the combination out loud."

"Well, I'd better be going," Tony said. "I'd sure like to have a game of Word Master with you sometime before the tournament, Carter."

Carter's shoulders relaxed a little. "I'd like that, Tony," he said. "Stop back anytime. I'll be here almost every day."

"Maybe on Saturday," Tony said. Then he left.

"How are you kids coming on those flyers?" Queenie asked.

"Pretty good," Benny said. "We've got a couple done. See?" He held them up to show Queenie, Carter and Raina.

"Those are beautiful!" Queenie exclaimed. "Aren't they beautiful, Carter?"

"They're okay," Carter said, barely glancing at them.

"Why don't you take them down to Bob's drugstore and make copies," Queenie suggested. "I'll give you some money." She opened the drawer, took out a couple of dollars, and handed them to Henry.

"In fact, while you're there, perhaps you can have a key made for Raina," Queenie added. "Would you mind?"

"Not at all," Jessie said.

"Let me just go into the back room and get the spare key," Queenie said.

While Henry, Jessie and Benny waited, they wandered back to check on the progress Violet had made. Her pencil marks were very light, so they had to get close to the wall to see.

"This is nice, Violet," Henry said.

"Thanks." Violet grinned.

Queenie came back with a frown on her face.

"What's the matter?" Carter asked her.

"You know that spare key I had hanging on a nail in the back room? It's gone!"

"Gone?" Carter repeated.

"You didn't take it, did you, Carter?" Queenie asked.

"No."

"How about you, Raina?" Queenie turned to the girl at the cash register.

"No." Raina shook her head. "But I remember seeing it there when I hung up my coat this morning."

"Hmm." Queenie's forehead wrinkled. "I wonder what happened to it? Well . . . ," She reached into her pocket and pulled out her own key. "Why don't you take this one and make two copies of it," she said, handing the key to Jessie.

"Okay," Jessie replied. Then she and Henry and Benny headed out the door.

"See? Now there's been more trouble at this mall," Benny said as the trio walked down to the drugstore. "Somebody took Queenie's key. Maybe this mall is bad luck!"

"There's no such thing as bad luck, Benny," Jessie said.

"And we don't know for sure that someone took it," Henry pointed out. "It may have just been misplaced."

"Maybe," Benny said. But he didn't think so. He opened the door to the drugstore. Bells jangled, announcing their arrival.

"Can I help you?" a man in a blue smock asked as he came toward them. He was tall and thin and the name tag on his smock said "Bob."

"We need to make copies of these papers," Jessie said, holding up the flyers they'd made. "And then we need two copies of this key, too." She held up the key.

"The copy machine is over there." Bob pointed. "And I can help you with the keys."

Jessie handed Henry the flyers so he could make the copies while she and Benny watched Bob grind the new keys.

When Bob finished with the keys, Jessie asked, "Could we also put up a flyer in here? Queenie is hosting a Word Master tournament at the Game Spot in a couple of weeks and she'd really like to get the word out."

"Sure," Bob replied. "You can leave one

with me and I'll put it up on the board in the entryway. But I have to warn you, if Carter Malone is playing, there may not be much response. Everyone knows Carter is an expert at word games."

"Yes, but it's fun just to play, even if you don't win," Jessie said.

"I guess you're right," Bob gave in. He handed Jessie the two keys. "Be careful with these now. You know there's been a robbery in this mall. You wouldn't want these keys to fall into the wrong hands."

"We'll be careful," Jessie promised. "Thanks."

CHAPTER 4

More Missing Letters

"Uh, oh," Benny said when he and Jessie and Henry came out of the drugstore a few minutes later.

"What's the matter, Benny?" Jessie asked.

"Look!" Benny pointed to the sign in the parking lot. "More letters are missing."

Benny was right. The sign that had read GRAND OPENING TODAY . . . THE GAME SPOT earlier this morning now read G_AND OP_NING . . . THE GAME SPOT.

"There's an R and an E missing," Henry

said as he shifted his stack of flyers from one hand to the other.

"Did either of you notice whether the letters were all there when we went into the drugstore?" Jessie asked.

"I didn't notice," Benny said.

"Neither did I," Henry said.

The children went back into the Game Spot. They handed Queenie the flyers and the spare keys, then told her about the sign. Violet heard what they were talking about and came over to see what was going on.

She and Queenie and Raina all stepped toward the window and peered outside.

"My goodness," Queenie said. "There are more letters missing. Raina, you've been working in the front of the store all day. Did you see anyone over by that sign?"

"No," Raina said. "But I wasn't looking, either."

"I wonder if Carter saw anything when he left?" Queenie asked. "It's hard to believe someone would take letters off that sign in the middle of the day."

"Why would someone take letters off

that sign any time?" Violet asked.

"I don't know," Henry replied. "Someone probably thinks they're being funny."

"Well, I know George won't be laughing when he hears about this," Queenie said. "He was just out here replacing letters."

"Why don't we go outside and see if we can find any clues," Henry suggested. "I'd like to find out who's taking letters off that sign."

"I would, too," Jessie said. "Is that okay with you, Queenie?"

"Sure. You children go right ahead."

So the Aldens went outside and walked across the parking lot. They searched the ground between the rosebushes and the sign, but they didn't find anything.

"Maybe we could go in the other stores and see if anyone saw anything?" Violet suggested.

"That's a good idea, Violet," Henry said.

So they went into the jewelry store next to the Game Spot first. There was only one employee in there, a well-dressed woman who smiled at them.

"I didn't see anything," the woman said. Her gold hoop earrings glimmered in the light. "But I've been busy getting ready for our sale this weekend. I haven't had time to be looking out the window."

"I don't know if anyone in the drugstore would have seen anything," Jessie said after they left the jewelry store. "The only employee I saw in there was the man who helped us. And he was busy with us the whole time."

"There might be other employees that we didn't see," Henry pointed out.

"And the letters could have been taken before we ever got to the drugstore," Benny put in.

"You're both right," Jessie said. So they went back into the drugstore.

Bob, the guy who had helped them before, was stamping price tags onto bottles of shampoo. "Hello," he smiled at the children. "You're back."

Jessie explained why they had returned.

"I didn't even know there were letters missing from that sign," Bob said. He waved toward his front door. "As you can see, I have so much stuff piled up around the windows, it's hard to see out."

"Thanks anyway," Henry said.

That only left the Java Café. Chip Douglas was at the counter when the children walked in. They could see that there wasn't a very good view of the sign from inside the coffee shop.

"I didn't see anything," Chip said. "But if something's missing, I suggest you pay close attention to that girl your friend Queenie hired. I still say Raina Holt is trouble."

"Raina's not trouble," Benny said, "She's nice."

Chip leaned closer to Benny. "Sometimes it's the nice ones you have to watch out for," he said.

Once the children were back outside, Jessie said, "Wow. Chip really doesn't like Raina very much, does he?"

"No, he doesn't," Henry said. "But he's pretty convinced she's the one who broke into his safe. You wouldn't like someone you thought had stolen from you, either."

"That's true," Jessie agreed. "But Raina's just so nice. It's hard to believe she's a thief."

"I agree," Henry said. "But then, if Raina didn't break into Chip's safe, who did?"

"That's a good question," Benny said.

* * * *

On Thursday, the Aldens dressed in their old clothes. Violet had finished her sketch, so it was time to start painting.

After a hearty breakfast of pancakes and fruit, Grandfather drove the children over to the Crossroads Mall. Once again there were some letters missing on the sign out front.

"Not again," Benny said, slumping back against his seat. The sign read:

20% OFF _ALE
AT _ _ _ _'S JEWEL_ _ STOR_

"The L, A, K, and E are missing, " Jessie said.

"Hey, *lake* is a word!" Benny said. "Do

you think someone might be taking letters so they can spell different words than what is on the sign?"

"I don't know, Benny," Henry replied. "Why would someone do that?"

"It might not be a bad idea to keep track of the letters that are taken," Jessie said. She leaned forward in her seat. "Do you have some paper and a pencil, Grandfather?"

Grandfather opened the glove compartment and pulled out a small pad of paper and a pen. He handed both to Jessie.

"Thanks," Jessie said, opening the notebook. She wrote down L, A, K, E.

"The R and the Y are missing in JEW-ELRY," Violet said.

"And the S is missing in SALE and the E is missing in STORE," Henry added.

Jessie added an R, Y, S and E to her list. Then she asked, "Does anybody remember what other letters have gone missing?"

"It was R and an E last time," Violet said.

Jessie nodded. "And I remember I re-placed the M and N in MONDAY and the P and O in SPOT," she said as she added those letters to her list.

"I added an E to THE and an A and E to GAME," Henry said.

"And if I remember right, the P, E, and I were missing in OPENING," Grandfather put in.

Jessie added those letters, too. The children stared at Jessie's list of letters: L A K E R Y S E R E M N P O E A E P E I. But they didn't see any pattern to them.

"We should get inside," Violet said. "We've got a lot of work to do today."

So the children said goodbye to Grandfather and went inside the store.

Raina was bustling around at the counter, picking things up and looking under them, then frowning as she set them down.

"Hi, Raina," the children greeted her.

"Oh. Hi, kids," Raina replied as she bent down, then stood back up. She tapped her fingers nervously against the counter.

"I—is something wrong, Raina?" Jessie asked.

Raina bit her lip. "Well, I wrote down a special order a little while ago, but I don't know what I did with the paper," she replied.

"I'm sure it'll turn up," Violet said.

As the children headed toward the Kids' Korner, they noticed Carter and Tony Silver sitting together at a table. A game of Word Master was spread out between them.

"Hey, Carter is supposed to be an expert at word games," Henry said. "I wonder if he would see any pattern to the letters that have been taken from the sign? That's kind of how you play Word Master."

Jessie shrugged. "I guess it doesn't hurt to ask him."

She pulled out her pad of paper and the children walked over to Carter and Tony.

The two men were in the middle of a conversation about the security of different kinds of safes.

"It's got to be solid steel construction," Carter said. "It's got to have three-quarter-inch diameter steel chromed locking bolts and reinforced internal jambs. Anything less shouldn't even be on the market."

"I agree," Tony said. "How do you know

so much about safes, Carter?"

"Oh, my father was a safe manufacturer," Carter said. "You could say it's in my blood." He smiled, but when he noticed the Aldens standing beside him, his smile fell.

"Sorry to bother you, Carter," Jessie said. "But you know someone has been taking letters from that sign out front, right?"

"Yes," Carter said impatiently. "What about it?"

"Well, we wrote down the letters that have gone missing. We know how good you are at word games, and we were wondering whether you might notice any pattern to these letters?"

Jessie held out the notebook for Carter to see, but he hardly looked at it. "I'm sure there's no pattern to those letters," he said gruffly. "The missing letters will probably turn up eventually." He brushed the notebook aside and turned back to the game in front of him.

"Would you please just take a quick look?" Benny begged.

Carter scowled. "Fine." He picked up

Jessie's notebook and glanced at it. "Sorry. I don't see anything. Now would you please let me get back to my game?"

"Sure," Jessie said. "We're sorry we bothered you."

The Aldens left Carter and Tony and went to look for Queenie. They found her in the back room mixing paint.

"Oh good. You're here," Queenie said when she noticed them standing there. "I put some old sheets down where you're going to be painting. And I got a bunch of brushes and all the paint colors you asked for. So I think we're set."

"Good," Violet said. "I can't wait to get started."

The older children each carried some paint. Benny carried the brushes. And Queenie followed behind with a six-pack of sodas. "In case you get thirsty," she said.

Once Queenie was sure the Aldens had everything they needed, she went up to the cash register to check on Raina.

"Did you ever find that special order, Raina?" Queenie asked.

Raina held up a scrap of paper. "Right here," she said with a smile. "I've already taken care of it."

"Good." Queenie nodded. "Then if you don't need me out here, I've got some paperwork to do in the back."

"That's fine," Raina said.

"We'll let you know if we need anything," Jessie said as she dipped her brush into a can of blue paint.

The Aldens spent the next hour painting. Benny painted triangle-shaped skirts on the girls and square-shaped pants and shirts on the boys. Jessie painted faces. Henry painted hair. And Violet outlined everything in black. Her picture was really coming to life.

"That's looking really nice, kids," Tony said when he and Carter finished their game.

"Yes, you're doing a nice job," Carter agreed.

"Thanks," Violet said, pleased to receive praise from Carter. He never seemed very friendly around them.

"Thanks for a good game, Carter," Tony said.

"My pleasure," Carter replied. Then he went to join Queenie in the back room.

Tony stopped at the front of the store and bought a pack of gum.

Raina was on the phone when she rang up Tony's gum. She had a very serious expression on her face. "Uh huh, I understand," she said into the phone. "That'll be sixty-five cents," she told Tony.

Tony handed Raina a dollar, and she put it in the cash register. "Yes, I'm still here," she said into the receiver.

Tony cleared his throat. "Uh, Raina? You forgot to give me my change."

Raina covered the phone again. "Oh, I'm sorry," she said, her face turning red. "Hang on a second," she told the person she was talking to on the phone. She punched in some buttons on the cash register and the drawer opened.

"What do I owe you?" Raina asked.

"Thirty five-cents," Tony replied.

Raina scooped up some coins and handed

them to Tony. "Here you go."

"Thanks," Tony said.

Once he was gone, Raina turned back to her phone conversation. She listened for a while, then said, "Yes, I know. I know! Look, I don't have the money now, but I can get it to you on Monday. Yes, Monday! I promise." Then she slammed the phone down.

"Is everything okay, Raina?" Jessie asked for the second time that day.

Raina jumped. "What? Oh yes. Everything's fine. I'm just a little behind on my rent. But I'll have money on Monday. Everything will be fine." She forced a smile, then hurried toward the back of the store.

"It seems like Raina's got some money problems," Violet said once Raina was gone.

"Yes, it does," Jessie agreed. "But it sounds like everything will be okay next week."

"I thought Queenie said she paid on the first and third Fridays of the month," Benny said.

"Yes, I think she said that when she hired Raina," Henry said.

"Today is only the second Friday of the month," Benny said, pointing to the calendar behind the cash register. "Queenie isn't paying today. And this is Raina's only job. So where is she going to get money on Monday?"

"I don't know," Jessie said. "But Raina's money problems really aren't any of our business."

"You're right, Jessie," Violet said. And the children got back to work.

CHAPTER 5

Message on the Sign

"How many words did you find, Benny?" Jessie asked on Sunday afternoon. A light rain was falling outside, so the Aldens were spending the day indoors. They were clustered around the kitchen table playing Word Master. The smell of baking cookies hung in the air.

"I found seven words," Benny said. "How many points is that?"

"It depends on which letters you used." Violet leaned over to count up Benny's points. "It looks like 75 points. Did you find the message in the words?"

"I don't think so," Benny said.

"How many points did you get, Violet?" Jessie asked, her pencil ready.

"I got 134 points," Violet replied. "I didn't find the message, either."

"I think I got the message," Henry said. "Is it 'good things come to those who wait?'"

"Yes," Jessie said.

"Then I got 154 points," Henry said.

"I got 128," Grandfather said.

Jessie was still counting her points. "I've got 162," she announced once she finished counting.

"Wow!" Violet said.

"Looks like you win again, Jessie," Grandfather said as he sat back in his chair.

The housekeeper, Mrs. McGregor, brought them a plate a freshly baked choco-late-chip cookies. "You all look like you could use a snack," she said as she set the plate in the middle of the table. "These just came out of the oven."

"Mm! That's the best time to have chocolate-chip cookies," Henry said, helping himself to two cookies.

"I'll go get the milk," Benny said, hopping down from his chair.

Violet went to get glasses and napkins. Then the Aldens slid back into their chairs and enjoyed their snack.

"Can I have that cookie?" Benny asked as he eyed the last cookie on the plate.

"Haven't you already had two cookies, Benny?" Jessie asked.

"Yes, but I'm still hungry."

Violet laughed. "You're always hungry."

"So?" Benny said.

"Go ahead, Benny," Grandfather said. "Then maybe we can divide up the letters for one more game."

"Okay," Benny said, snatching the last cookie.

Violet and Grandfather turned over all the letters and started handing them out.

"Can we play in the Word Master tournament, Grandfather?" Violet asked.

"I don't know why not," Grandfather replied. "I'm sure you'll all do quite well."

In the middle of the second round, the phone rang. Mrs. McGregor picked it up. "Alden residence," she said. "What? Oh, no!"

The Aldens all turned when they heard the concern in Mrs. McGregor's voice.

"I'll let you talk to James, Queenie," Mrs. McGregor said. She handed the phone to Grandfather.

"What's happened, Mrs. McGregor?" Jessie asked.

"Are there more letters missing from that sign?" Benny asked.

"It's worse than that," Mrs. McGregor said, wringing her hands together. "I'd rather let your grandfather tell you about it."

So the children waited for Grandfather to get off the phone.

"We'll be there as soon as we can," Grandfather said. Then he hung up.

"I'm afraid I've got some bad news," he said as he stood up and reached for his coat. "The Game Spot is closed on Sundays, but Queenie went in anyway this afternoon to catch up on some paperwork. It's a good thing she did. Otherwise she wouldn't have known until tomorrow that . . . her store has been robbed."

* * * *

The police were just leaving the Game Spot when the Aldens arrived.

"Did they find anything?" Grandfather asked.

"Unfortunately, no," Queenie replied. Carter was standing right behind her. They both stepped aside so the Aldens could enter.

"It's just like what happened at the Java Café last week," Queenie explained. "The store was locked when I came in. There's nothing else out of place. The only thing missing is the money I had in the safe."

Queenie led the group back to the back room. A small metal safe sat in the corner. The door stood open, and the safe was empty.

The Aldens wandered around the room

looking for clues, but there seemed to be nothing out of the ordinary. There was no dirt or mud on the carpet. The papers piled on Queenie's desk had been untouched. There was even a gold watch on Queenie's desk that was still there. Piles of games and puzzles that hadn't been put out for sale yet lined the shelves. Clearly, whoever had been back here had only been interested in one thing: the money inside Queenie's safe.

"What about fingerprints?" Henry asked. "Did the police find any fingerprints?"

Carter shook his head. "The front door, the door to this back room and the safe had all been wiped down. Whoever came in here was wearing gloves."

"Somebody had to have had a key to this store and the combination to this safe," Queenie said as she paced back and forth. "They unlocked the front door, walked back here, opened the safe, then left again, locking the front door behind them."

"Who could have done that?" Grandfather asked.

"I don't know," Queenie replied.

"What about that key you were missing the other day?" Violet asked. "Did you ever find it?"

"I'm afraid not," Queenie said.

Carter frowned. "We probably don't want to leave a spare key hanging on a nail in the back room anymore, Queenie. It was convenient for us, but anybody who went back there could have grabbed it."

"But nobody goes back there besides us," Queenie said.

"We've had all kinds of people back there this past week," Carter said. "Workers and delivery people. Any of them could have taken it."

"But they would have had to know the combination to the safe to get into it," Queenie said. "Remember, I changed it this week. The only people who knew the new combination are the people who are here right now."

"And that young woman you hired," Carter said. "Raina Holt."

The Aldens exchanged a look. Raina again.

Queenie pressed her lips together. "Raina did not do this, Carter. She wasn't even working yesterday. She was visiting a friend out of town."

"I hope you're not making a mistake trusting her so completely, Queenie," Carter replied.

"Hey!" Benny said all of a sudden. He walked over to the window. "Look at that sign now!"

In their rush to get to the store, the Aldens hadn't noticed the sign on their way in. But they could see now that it had been altered again. This time there weren't any letters missing. Instead there were two words in the middle of the sign. All the other letters had been crammed together around the edges as though they weren't needed.

The two words were CARTER and ROBBER.

Carter's face turned bright red. "Is this some kind of joke?" he roared. He turned to the Aldens. "Did you kids rearrange those letters?"

"No," they all responded in unison.

"I didn't notice that sign earlier today," Queenie spoke up. "But I know that yesterday it said CALL GEORGE BERBER TO RENT AT THE CROSSROADS MALL."

Carter banged the door open and strode across the parking lot. The Aldens stood in the doorway to the Game Spot with Queenie and watched as he yanked down all the letters that spelled CARTER and ROBBER. When he came back into the store, he threw the letters down onto the counter.

"I know you didn't have anything to do with these robberies, Carter," Queenie said, trying to calm him down.

"Well, somebody thinks I did," Carter said.

"That or someone's trying to make it look like you did," Henry pointed out.

"Who would do such a thing?" Queenie asked.

"I don't know," Jessie replied. "Perhaps the real robber?"

"I wish we knew who that was," Queenie said.

Later, when the children were back home, they went out to the boxcar in the backyard to talk more about the case.

"Do you think Carter really is innocent? Or do you think someone is trying to tell us something by writing CARTER and ROBBER on that sign?" Henry asked.

"I don't know," Jessie said as she stretched her legs out and leaned back against the wall of the boxcar. "That's a good question. Is the person who is taking letters off the sign is the same person who is breaking into the safes?"

"That's another good question," Henry said.

"Well, what do we know about Carter?" Jessie asked.

"We know he works at the Game Spot with Queenie," Violet said. "And the two of them seem to be pretty close friends."

"We know he has a key to the Game Spot and that he knew the combination to the safe," Benny added.

"But he wouldn't have had a key to the Java Café," Jessie said. "And he wouldn't have known the combination to their safe."

"Probably not," Henry agreed. "But he knows something about safes. Remember, he said his father was a safe manufacturer?"

"That's right," Jessie said.

"Maybe the Java Café and the Game Spot were robbed by different people," Violet said.

"Maybe," Jessie said. "But you know, there is somebody who had a key to both stores and who knew the combination to both safes."

"Raina," Henry and Violet said at the same time.

"We also know that Raina needed money," Jessie said.

"But Queenie said Raina was out of town yesterday," Benny said.

"And if Raina is the robber, then why didn't the sign out front say RAINA and ROBBER instead of CARTER and ROBBER?" Violet asked.

"Maybe Raina's the one who wrote the

message," Jessie said. "Maybe she's trying to frame Carter."

"Maybe," Henry said. "But Queenie is sure that both Carter and Raina are innocent."

"And maybe they are," Violet said. "Maybe the robber is someone else entirely."

"Maybe," Henry said. "We don't have enough evidence to accuse anybody yet. But I think we should keep an eye on both Carter and Raina and see if either of them do anything suspicious."

Jessie nodded. "Good idea, Henry. And let's not forget George Berber, either. Remember, he has a key to both stores."

"But did he know the combinations to the safes?" Violet asked.

"I don't know," Henry said. "But that would be a good thing to find out."

CHAPTER 6

The Figure in the Night

On Monday morning, the Aldens put on their old clothes again and biked over to the Crossroads Mall. They were planning to do some more work on the mural.

"Hey, the sign is blank today," Violet said as they rode into the mall parking lot.

"That's strange," Jessie said. "I wonder if someone took all the letters this time or if there just wasn't a message on the sign this morning."

The children locked their bikes at the

bike rack, then headed over to the Game Spot.

A van that said SILVER'S SAFES on the side was parked in front of Lake's Jewelry Store next to the Game Spot.

"I wonder if they're getting a new safe at the jewelry store?" Violet said.

"I wouldn't be surprised," Jessie said, opening the door. "Now that there have been two robberies in this mall, other store owners are probably getting worried. They want to make sure their safes are secure."

When the children stepped inside the store they found Queenie and Carter in the middle of a serious conversation with George Berber, the mall owner. The three of them were seated around the table.

The Aldens didn't want to intrude, but they didn't want to start on the mural without permission from Queenie, either. So they lingered over by the model train set.

"You're the store owner, Queenie," George was saying. "You tell me what you want that sign to say. As long as I've got the letters, you can say whatever you want to say.

Queenie glanced at Carter. "I don't know. I like STOP IN AND SEE GREEN-FIELD'S NEWEST GAME STORE. I don't need my name up there on that sign for the whole world to see."

"Yes, but you're trying to project an image of small-town friendliness," Carter said. "I think STOP IN AND SAY HELLO TO QUEENIE AT THE GAME SPOT sounds so much nicer. And it'll be good for business."

Queenie thought about it for a moment. "Well, if you really think it's a good idea, Carter," she said finally. She turned to George. "Okay, go ahead and write STOP IN AND SAY HELLO TO QUEENIE AT THE GAME SPOT."

"I'll have to see if I've got enough *E*s left for that whole message," George said as he rifled through his letters. "Let's see—one, two, three, four, five, six. You're in luck. I have just enough."

"Oh good," Queenie said.

George and Queenie both stood up. "I'll get your message up right away. I just hope the letters don't go missing as soon as the message is put up."

Queenie said good bye to George, then walked over to the Aldens. She looked tired today.

"Hello, kids," she said. "I'm afraid what with all the commotion yesterday I haven't been able to get out and get you some more paint."

"Oh, that's okay," Jessie said. "Would you like us to come back another time?"

"Would you mind?" Queenie asked. "Perhaps I could leave Raina in charge of the store and go out later this afternoon?"

"Would you like us to stick around in case Raina needs help while you're gone?" Violet offered.

"Oh no," Queenie replied. "That won't be necessary. Raina can handle things just fine. And if for some reason she can't, Carter should be here, too."

"What can I handle?" Raina asked as she came up behind them with a stack of games in her hands. A pretty sapphire necklace lay against her throat.

Queenie jumped. "Oh, Raina. I didn't see you there. I was just telling the Aldens that I'm going to try and get to the paint store this afternoon. You can handle things by yourself, can't you?"

"Certainly," Raina replied. She set the games on the shelf behind her.

"Good," Queenie said. "Because I'd like to get that Kids' Korner finished by this weekend. Do you suppose your grandfather would let you come to paint this evening while the store is closed?"

The children all glanced at one another. "I'm sure he will," Henry said.

"Good." Queenie smiled. "Then I'll see you all tonight. Shall we say seven o'clock?"

"Seven o'clock it is," Jessie said.

As the children were leaving, they noticed Raina twisting her finger around her necklace while she spoke to Carter.

"That's a beautiful necklace, Raina," Carter said. "Where did you get it?"

"At Lake's Jewelry Store next door,"

Raina replied with a sheepish smile. "I really don't have the money to be buying myself jewelry. But I saw it in the window this morning. And it was on sale, so I just couldn't resist."

Carter glanced over his shoulder nervously. "Do they have a lot of nice things?" he asked in a low voice. "I've never been in there."

"Oh, yes," Raina said enthusiastically. "Lots of nice things. You should stop in sometime."

"Maybe I'll stop in there right now," Carter said. "Thanks, Raina." He turned to Queenie and said, "I'm going to step out for a few minutes, okay?"

"Sure, Carter," Queenie replied. "When you get back, I think I'll go over to the paint store."

The Aldens followed Carter out. They watched as he went into the jewelry store next door. Tony's truck was gone.

"I wonder where Raina got the money for that necklace?" Jessie said. "She was pretty low on money last Friday."

"Well, she told the person she was talking to on the phone that she was going to get paid today. Maybe Queenie gave her a paycheck early," Henry suggested.

"Maybe," Jessie said.

"Hey, George is still here!" Henry pointed across the parking lot to where the mall owner was placing letters on the sign. "This is a good time to talk to him."

By the time the Aldens got across the parking lot, George was almost finished.

"Hey, kids," George said as he closed up his book of plastic letters.

"It's too bad someone keeps stealing the letters from your sign," Violet said.

"Yes, it is," George agreed. "These are the last E*s* I have. If they disappear, too, I don't know what I'll do."

"It's too bad about the safe robberies, too," Henry said. "Do the police have any leads?"

"None at all," George said with a heavy sigh. "And that's bad news, too. People hear about the robberies and they don't want to rent space in this mall. Look at all the storefronts that are still empty." He gestured toward the mall.

"There have to be some clues somewhere," Jessie said. "Someone had a key to both the Java Café and the Game Spot and someone knew the combinations to both safes. It shouldn't be so hard to find out who that could be."

"Chip Douglas and Raina Holt were the only people who had keys to the Java Café, and they were the only people who knew the combination to that safe. And Queenie Polk, Carter Malone and Raina Holt were the only people who had keys to the Game Spot and the only people who knew the combination to the safe there."

"Everything seems to be pointing to Raina," Jessie noted.

"But Queenie has known Raina since she was a little girl," Violet pointed out. "She's sure Raina isn't guilty."

"The police don't think she's involved, either," George said as he stopped in front of a white jeep. "They checked out her story. Apparently she really was out of town when this last robbery occurred."

"What about you?" Benny asked boldly. "Don't you have a key to both stores and don't you know the combinations to both safes?"

"Benny!" Jessie exclaimed. It sounded like Benny was accusing George of something.

But George just smiled good-naturedly. "That's okay, Jessie. I have nothing to hide. I do have a key to both stores. In fact, I have a key to all the stores here. I need to be able to get in in case there's an emergency. But I don't know the combinations to any of the safes."

"I hope you don't think we were accusing you," Jessie said. "We're just trying to gather information."

"I know," George said. "And I appreciate that you kids are trying to find our robber."

"I just wish we were having better luck," Henry said.

* * * *

That night the Aldens returned to the Game Spot at seven o'clock as planned. Queenie had gotten to the paint store and picked up all the colors they had requested. She had also bought a wooden table and four chairs for the Kids' Korner.

"I couldn't find tables and chairs in bright colors," Queenie explained. "Are you still willing to paint these?"

"Absolutely," Violet said. "We can use the tables and chairs to bring out the colors in the mural."

"That's a wonderful idea," Queenie said. "I'm really pleased with the job you kids are doing."

"Thanks," Violet replied. "We're having fun, too."

"Well, I can see you don't need me, so if you don't mind, I'll be working in the back-room," Queenie said.

"Okay," Jessie said.

The children got their paint and supplies. They spread out dropcloths below where they were working. Then they got busy. Jessie and Violet did some small brush work around the mural. Benny and Henry worked on the table.

"What do you think, Benny?" Henry asked. "Red or yellow?"

"Yellow," Benny replied. "With a blue lightning strike down the middle."

"That sounds good!" Henry said. He opened a can of yellow paint and started stirring.

It was so quiet in the store that night that Queenie had put on a radio for background noise. Every now and then the children would sing along with a song they recognized. But other than that, they worked straight for the next hour.

"Whew!" Jessie wiped the back of her hand across her forehead. "I'm ready for a break."

"Me, too," Henry said. He and Benny had just finished painting the table yellow. They'd need to let the paint dry before adding the blue lightning strike.

It was starting to get dark outside. The streetlights in the parking lot had come on.

"Shall we go wash our hands and get a

snack?" Jessie asked. Mrs. McGregor had packed them some cheese and crackers and lemonade in case they got hungry while they were working.

"Sure," Violet said.

One by one, the children took turns washing up in the small bathroom in the back, then they went to sit down at the large table in the front of the store.

"The mural is almost done," Violet said. "And I don't think it'll take very long to paint those chairs. We'll probably just need to come in one more time to finish all that up."

"Hooray!" Benny said. "I can't wait until the Kids' Korner is done!"

"I bet Jessie can't, either," Henry said. "She'll be in here all the time playing Word Master."

Violet and Benny nodded their agreement.

But Jessie didn't seem to be paying much attention to what they were saying. She was staring at something out the window.

"What are you looking at, Jessie?" Violet

asked. It was getting dark outside, so it was hard to see anything.

"I don't know," Jessie replied, her forehead pressed against the glass. "I thought I saw someone moving around in the bushes in front of that sign out there, but I'm not seeing anything now. Maybe I was mistaken."

The others all pressed their hands to the window and peered out into the darkness, too.

"I just saw something, too," Henry said.

"So did I," Benny said. "It looks like there's someone hiding in the rose bushes. I think they're reaching up and taking letters off the sign."

"Let's go!" Henry leaped to his feet. "Maybe we can catch our letter thief in the act."

CHAPTER 7

Another Robbery

The Aldens raced out the front door and across the parking lot. But the noise they were making alerted the intruder, and he dashed away in the opposite direction.

All they could see was that he was tall and thin and wore jeans and a jacket. He ran around behind the mall. The children hurried after him. But when they reached the back alley, they found it deserted.

"Where did he go?" Henry asked, glancing left, then right.

The intruder was nowhere in sight.

"Where do all these doors go?" Benny asked. "Could he have gone inside one of them?"

"I think those doors all lead to the different stores in the mall," Jessie said as she rested against the brick building. "He could have gone inside one of them."

Henry tried the door closest to them. "It's locked," he said.

The children continued down the alley, trying each door along the way. But they were all locked.

There was a fence at the end of the alley. The intruder may have climbed the fence, or, if he had a key, he may have gone inside one of the doors. Either way, he was gone.

Disappointed, the Aldens turned around and walked back around to the front of the mall.

"Did anyone get a good look at him?" Jessie asked.

"No. It was too dark," Violet said.

Queenie was pacing back and forth on the sidewalk. "My goodness," she said when she saw the children. "I heard you all go running out of the store, but I didn't know where you went. I was worried."

"We're sorry," Violet said. "We didn't mean to worry you. But we saw somebody pulling letters off that sign. We wanted to see if we could catch him."

"And did you catch him?" Queenie asked hopefully.

Benny shook his head. "He was too fast."

"Which letters did he take this time?" Jessie asked.

The group walked over so they could read the sign. The children remembered that the sign was supposed to say STOP IN AND SAY HELLO TO QUEENIE AT THE GAME SPOT. Now it said STOP IN AND SAY HEL_O TO _ _EENIE AT THE GA_E SPOT.

"There's an L, a Q, a U, and an M missing," Violet said.

"Hey, what's this?" Benny reached for a piece of brown cloth that was stuck to a thorn on one of the rosebushes in front of the sign.

"Looks like part of a pocket," Jessie said as she fingered the cloth.

"Do you suppose our intruder could have lost it in his rush to get out of here?" Henry asked.

"Maybe," Violet said.

Benny handed the cloth to Henry, and he put it in his pocket.

* * * *

The next day, when the Aldens arrived at the Game Spot to finish up the painting, they were greeted with more bad news.

"The jewelry store was broken into last night," Raina told the children.

"Oh, no," Jessie groaned. "Not another robbery!" She noticed Queenie and Carter standing off to the side talking with George. She moved closer to hear what they were saying.

"Why is this thief targeting my mall?" George demanded as he banged his fist on the table. "There haven't been any other robberies in town. All the robberies have been here."

"And they've all involved safes," Carter pointed out. "I wonder if there's something wrong with these safes? Maybe we should get Tony to come out here and take a look."

"Was there anything else taken from the jewelry store?" Henry asked.

"No," Queenie replied. "It was just like the robbery here and the one at the Java Café. There was no forced entry. Nothing else out of place. The store owner came in this morning and found the safe door standing wide open and its contents emptied."

"It sounds like whoever the thief is, he's good at picking locks," Jessie said. "He was able to get into the stores, and then he was able to get into the safes."

"Well, he may not have had to pick locks to get into the stores," Queenie said. "He may have been able to get in with keys. Remember, I told you I was missing that key? It turns out Sandra next door was also missing a spare key. She kept it on her desk. But she noticed yesterday that it was missing. And then last night her store was broken into."

"That's interesting," Jessie said. "Was there a spare key missing from the Java Café?" she asked Raina.

Raina blinked. "I-I really don't know," she stammered. "I don't know where Chip kept his spare key."

Just then a young couple walked into the store.

"I'll go see if they need some help," Raina said as she hurried over to them.

"Why don't we go down to the Java Café and ask Chip whether he's missing any keys," Violet suggested.

"Yes, let's," Benny said.

So the Aldens walked down to the Java Café at the end of the mall. There was a businessman reading a newspaper while Chip mixed a coffee drink.

"Here you go," Chip said as he handed the paper cup to the businessman.

"Thanks." The man nodded at Chip, then

picked up his drink and went to sit down.

The children stepped up to the counter.

"Can I help you kids?" Chip asked, as he started wiping the counter.

"Did you know there were keys missing both at the Game Spot and at Lake's Jewelry Store before they were robbed?" Violet asked.

Chip stopped wiping. "No, I didn't."

"We were just wondering whether there were any keys missing here before this store was robbed?" Henry asked.

Chip frowned. "There were a couple of them missing," he said. "Raina Holt only worked for me for ten days, but in that time she managed to lose two keys."

"Are you sure she lost them?" Henry asked. "They didn't just disappear?"

"No, she's the one who lost them," Chip insisted. "I had to get new keys made twice."

"I wonder why she didn't mention that when we asked her about missing keys," Jessie said.

"Maybe she was embarrassed?" Violet suggested.

"Or maybe she's the thief," Chip said.

"The police don't think so," Jessie said. "She was out of town when the Game Spot was robbed."

"She had a key to this place and she had a key to the Game Spot," Henry said. "But she wouldn't have had a key to the jewelry store."

"Maybe she managed to get one," Chip said. "She's a smooth one. She's got you all fooled. But I'm warning you. As long as that girl continues to work in this mall, there will continue to be robberies here. You mark my words."

The Aldens took their time walking back to the Game Spot.

"No matter what anyone tells him, Chip just will not believe that Raina is innocent," Violet said.

"Well, she was in the jewelry store yesterday," Jessie pointed out. "Remember? She bought herself that necklace. But that doesn't mean she stole a key to the store."

The children stopped just outside the

Game Spot door. "Lots of people were probably in there yesterday," Violet said. "Including Carter. But I agree with you. I don't know how either of them could have gotten the key from the back room."

"Unless they snuck back there when no one was looking," Benny said.

"That's certainly possible," Violet said.

"Hey Jessie," Henry said. "Are you still keeping track of the letters that are missing from that sign?"

"Yes. I have the list right here." She patted her pocket.

"Why don't we go inside and take a look at it," Henry suggested. "Maybe there's a clue in those letters?"

So they went inside the Game Spot and sat down at the main table. Jessie took out her list of letters and added the new ones to the list. Violet went to get some paper, a pencil and a pair of scissors. Then the children copied down all the letters onto four sheets of paper:

L A K E R Y S E R E M N
P O E A E P E I L Q U M

Then they cut out the letters and each of them took a set.

"Let's see how many words we can find in these letters," Jessie said as she started moving the letters around in front of her.

Benny found PLAY and ME. Violet found PLEASE. Jessie found SAME and MAPLE. Henry found MERRY and MARRY.

"Hey, I see Queenie's name," Violet squealed. She pulled out the Q U E E N - I E and the P O L K and lined them up in front of her.

"What are you kids doing?" Carter asked, his jaw set tight.

Jessie jumped. She hadn't realized he was standing over her shoulder.

"We're trying to make words," Benny said.

"These are all the letters that have been taken from the sign out front," Jessie explained. "We're looking to see if there's a message in here."

Carter's eyes narrowed. "Don't you kids have work to do?"

"Well . . . ," Violet glanced nervously at the others. Carter was right; they were supposed to be painting. That was why they were here.

Carter reached across the table and scooped up all their letter scraps into his hand. "You promised to paint the Kids' Korner today," he said, squeezing the scraps of paper in his fist. "So I think Queenie would really appreciate it if you got to work."

"Sure. Okay," the children said as they stood up.

Carter sprinkled the scraps of paper into the trash can, then went to the back room.

"Why is Carter so mad at us?" Benny asked. "We're just trying to help."

"You're right, Benny," Jessie said as she put a protective arm around her brother. "I don't know why he got so mad."

Was he really worried about them keeping their promise to Queenie or was there another reason he was upset?

CHAPTER 8

A Perfect Match

The next day, the Aldens decided to look at the missing letters again at home. They sat at the kitchen table. Once again, each of them had the letters A A E E E E E I K L L M M N O P P Q R R S U and Y spread out on scraps of paper in front of them.

"This is like playing Word Master," Benny said. "Except we have more letters."

"It's like a more challenging version of Word Master," Violet said as she moved the letters around.

Jessie kept a list of all the words they'd found in those letters. The list included QUEENIE, POLK, PLAY, ME, PLEASE, SAME, MAPLE, MERRY, MARRY, MY, PEARL, SALE, SEAL, MEAL, SPRAY, and YES. But so far the children hadn't found any message in the words. And they still didn't know how Queenie's name might fit in.

While they were working, Grandfather came into the room. "I'm afraid Mrs. Mc-Gregor isn't feeling well this morning," he said.

"Oh, no," Violet said with concern. "What's wrong?"

"Nothing serious," Grandfather said right away. "She just has a sore throat. But I was wondering whether you kids would mind running to the drugstore to get some throat drops for her? She's got enough for today, but if she's still not feeling well to-morrow, she's going to need some more."

"Sure," Henry said, rising from his chair. "We'll go right now."

"Let's go to the drugstore at Crossroads

Mall," Jessie said. "Then we can see if any more letters have been removed."

"That's a good idea," Henry said.

"Tell Mrs. McGregor I hope she feels better soon," Benny told Grandfather on his way out the door.

"I will," Grandfather replied. "And if you'd like to stop in at the Game Spot and say hello to Queenie while you're out, that's fine. Just be home in time for lunch."

"We will," Violet promised.

The children hopped on their bikes and rode to the mall. The sign out front was blank again.

"I hope that means nobody has taken any more letters," Violet said.

The children locked their bikes at the bike rack, then went inside the drugstore. They found Tony Silver standing at the counter talking with Bob, the same employee who had helped the Aldens a few days ago. A tool box sat on the floor beside Tony.

"Hi, Tony," Jessie said. "I didn't see your truck out front."

"Oh, I'm parked around back." Tony smiled at Jessie. "Bob here asked me to come and replace his safe."

"I just wasn't sure my other safe was really secure," Bob said. "All the robberies around here have me a little concerned. My store is the only one in the whole mall that hasn't been hit."

"Well, this is the sturdiest safe on the market," Tony said. "I don't think you'll be having any trouble."

"I hope not," Bob said.

Tony leaned against the counter. "Do the police have any leads on these robberies?"

"It doesn't sound like it," Bob replied. "Whoever it is must be a real pro."

"Did they check out that guy from the game store?" Tony asked. "What's his name again? Carter?"

"Yes," Henry said. "Carter Malone. But I don't know that anyone's really considered him a suspect."

"I don't know. I've seen him prowling around here at night," Tony said. "I asked him what he was doing and he said he was just taking a walk. But who walks around the mall after it's closed?"

"Apparently, Carter does," Bob replied. "I've seen him, too. But that doesn't mean he's a robber."

"Did you see that sign in the parking lot the other day?" Tony asked. "It said CARTER and ROBBER. Maybe someone knows something the rest of us don't know?"

"Or maybe someone's trying to frame Carter," Henry said.

"Could be," Tony admitted. "But I have to tell you, I was playing a game with him the other day and there's something a little different about him. Plus he sure knows a lot about safes. More than the average person should know."

"Well, the police are looking into it," Bob said as he wiped the counter. "Did you kids need something?"

"We need some throat drops for our housekeeper," Jessie said.

"I better let you get back to work," Tony said to Bob. He picked up his toolbox, then went out through the back of the store.

Bob led the children over to an aisle that contained cold and flu supplies. "These should do the trick," he said, pulling a bag of red drops off the rack.

"Thanks," Henry said. "We'll take them."

The children paid for the throat drops, then left.

Violet seemed especially quiet.

"What are you thinking about, Violet?" Jessie asked.

Violet frowned. "I don't know. I was just thinking that every time Tony puts in a safe at this mall, that store gets robbed."

Henry thought back to when the jewelry store and Queenie's store were robbed. "Hmm. You're right, Violet."

"What are you saying?" Jessie asked. "Do you think Tony is the thief?"

"He would certainly know all the combinations to the safes," Benny pointed out.

"And he could've stolen keys when he brought the safes into the stores," Henry added.

"But he seems like such a nice man,"

Violet said. "I hate to think of him robbing his customers."

"Still, he's probably our best suspect at this point," Jessie said. "Maybe we should keep an eye on the drugstore tonight? See if he, or anyone else, tries to sneak back in and rob the store after closing."

"That's a good idea, Jessie," Henry said. "Let's talk to Grandfather about that when we get home."

* * * *

Before heading home, the children decided to stop in at the Game Spot and see how their mural looked now that the paint was dry. When they arrived, they found Queenie and Raina decorating the store for next week's big Word Master tournament. Carter was seated at the main table. His brown jacket was draped over a chair. He was too engrossed in the papers in front of him to pay any attention to the children.

But Queenie greeted them cheerfully.

"Well, hello there. I wasn't expecting to see you children today."

"We thought we'd stop in and take a look at the mural," Jessie explained.

"I'm glad you did," Queenie said. She set the Word Master flyer and the stapler down on a chair. "It turned out so nicely! I spent the morning getting the table and chairs arranged and putting the pillows down. And now I think the Kids' Korner is officially done."

They all walked to the Kids'Korner. Red, blue and green chairs sat around a yellow table in the middle of an open area that had been partitioned off from the rest of the store. Large, fluffy pillows were stacked in a corner next to some games. And the mural on the wall showed a variety of children standing in a line holding hands. The whole area looked really inviting.

"This is wonderful, Queenie," Violet cried.

Queenie shrugged. "Well, you kids did most of the work. I'm pleased with how things turned out. Now the children who come in here have someplace to play while their parents look at games or play a game of their own."

"Could we play a game here right now?" Benny asked.

"I don't see why not," Queenie replied. "What game would you like to play?"

"How about Word Master?" Jessie suggested.

"That's a good idea," Queenie said. "You can practice for the tournament next week. You kids are planning to play in the tournament, aren't you?"

"We sure are," Jessie said.

"Wonderful," Queenie said as she went to get a copy of Word Master off the shelf. She set it on the table in front of the children. "Carter's really taking this tournament seriously. He's been studying word lists all week."

"Wow, he must really like to win," Henry said.

"He likes to do his best," Queenie said.

Benny opened up the Word Master box, and Violet and Jessie started dividing up the letters. Queenie went back to hanging flyers.

While the children were playing, Carter suddenly stood up. He picked up his brown jacket and put it on. As he did, Violet noticed that part of his pocket was torn off.

Violet nudged Jessie. "Look at Carter's jacket," she whispered.

Jessie turned. "Hey, the pocket is torn all the way off," she replied in a low voice.

Henry reached into his jacket pocket and pulled out the scrap of cloth they'd found in the rose bushes the other night.

"Carter's jacket is the same color as this cloth," Henry said.

"I'm going to go down to the drugstore and get a newspaper," Carter told Queenie as he straightened his jacket.

"Okay," Queenie called back. "I'll see you in a little bit."

"Quick! Let's get this game picked up," Jessie said. "We need to talk to Carter about his jacket."

The Aldens quickly scooped up the letters and put them back in the box. Violet closed up the box and put it back on the shelf.

"Let's not tell Queenie what we're doing until we talk to Carter," Henry said.

"Good idea," Jessie said. "We don't want to upset her until we know something for sure."

The children put on their jackets and hurried toward the front of the store.

"We're going to head out, too, Queenie," Henry said with a wave.

"Okay. Thanks for stopping in," Queenie said.

When they got outside, they noticed Carter was just going inside the drugstore. The children decided to wait outside the store for him.

"I wonder why Carter would take letters off that sign?" Benny said. "What is he doing with them?"

"We'll ask him that, Benny," Henry said.

"And if he's the one who has been taking the letters off the sign, why would he leave a message that says CARTER ROBBER?" Violet wondered.

"That is strange," Jessie said. She reached into her pocket and pulled out the list of words they'd found in the missing letters. "Let's look again and see if we can find a message in these words while we wait for Carter."

The others crowded around Jessie and looked at the paper in her hand. QUEE-NIE, POLK, PLAY, ME, PLEASE, SAME, MAPLE, MERRY, MARRY, MY, PEARL, SALE, SEAL, MEAL, SPRAY, and YES.

"'Please play with me' . . ." Violet said.

"No, there's no W, T or H," Jessie said.

"'Sale please' . . ." Henry said.

"'Please Queenie' . . . ," Benny said.

"Now what are you kids doing?" Carter asked in a gruff voice. He had a newspaper tucked under his arm.

"We're trying to figure out why you would have taken all those letters off that sign," Jessie announced.

"What are you talking about?" Carter asked.

Henry held up the fabric scrap for Carter to see. Up close, there was no doubt it matched Carter's jacket perfectly.

Carter glanced around nervously. "Look, it's not what you think," he said in a low voice. "How about we go down to that coffee shop and I'll explain everything."

CHAPTER 9

The Secret Message

The children followed Carter down to the Java Café. Carter went to the counter and ordered everyone cookies and hot chocolate. Then they all took their treats to a large table in the back of the café.

"I have been taking letters off that sign," Carter admitted. "But it's not what you think. I'm planning on giving the letters back. When I'm finished with them."

"What are you doing with them?" Henry asked.

Benny took a bite of his cookie and listened intently.

"You were on the right track when you were looking for a message in the missing letters," Carter explained. "I've been trying to collect the right letters so I can spell out a message."

"You want to spell out a message on the mall sign?" Jessie asked. "Why?"

Carter smiled. "If you knew what the message was, I think you'd understand." He reached inside the inner pocket of his jacket, pulled out a stack of plastic letters and laid them all out on the table.

"What is the message supposed to say?" Benny asked.

"Let's see if you can figure it out," Carter said. "I've finally collected all the letters I need."

The Aldens watched as Carter moved some of the letters around on the table. "These letters make up the first word," Carter said as he separated out the letters L E P E A S.

Jessie moved the six letters around until

she found the word. "The word is PLEASE," she said.

"That's right," Carter said. He pulled five more letters out of the pile: R A R M Y.

Henry scratched his head. "The word isn't army," he said. "There would be an R left over."

"That's right," Carter said, taking a sip of hot chocolate. "Keep looking. You'll get it."

Violet moved the M to the front of the word. She grinned. "I know what the word is. It's MARRY!"

Carter nodded. "And you already know that Queenie's first and last names are in here." He pulled out the Q U E E N I E and P O L K and laid the letters out at the end of the table.

"That's why you talked Queenie into changing the message on the sign that day," Jessie said. "You needed those letters."

"That's right," Carter said.

"That only leaves M and E," Benny said, reaching for the last two letters. "That spells ME." He inserted the word in its proper place.

The children read the message in full: PLEASE MARRY ME QUEENIE POLK.

"I'm planning to put that message up tonight after dark," Carter explained. "That way Queenie will see it when she comes in in the morning. Would you kids like to help me put it up?"

"Oh, yes," Violet said eagerly. The others agreed.

"Everyone was right about you kids," Carter said. "You are good detectives. I'm just glad that it was you who figured out what I was doing instead of Queenie."

"Well, don't worry," Jessie said. "We won't tell her."

"But there's still something I don't understand," Benny said, his face wrinkled in confusion.

"What's that?" Carter asked.

"If you're the one who's been messing up the sign, why would you rearrange the letters to say CARTER ROBBER?" Benny asked. "You're not the safe robber, are you?"

Carter stiffened. "No, I'm not," he said.

"And I'm not the one who put that message there. I wish I knew who did."

Jessie finished the last of her hot chocolate, then wiped her mouth with her napkin. "I wonder if it was the real robber?"

"There have been three robberies here and the police still don't have any leads," Carter said. "I don't suppose you kids have any idea who the robber is?"

"We have an idea," Henry said.

"Who?" Carter asked.

"Well," Jessie said. "Raina had a key to the Java Café and to the Game Spot. And she knew the combinations to both safes. But she didn't have a key to the jewelry store. And she was out of town when the Game Spot was robbed. So we don't think she could have done it."

"And George has a key to all three stores, but he said he didn't know any of the combinations to the safes," Violet explained. "Plus it wouldn't make sense for him to steal from his own tenants. They'd go out of business and then his mall would sit empty."

"Then there's Tony Silver," Benny said.

"The guy who installs the safes?" Carter asked.

"We don't know for sure that he's our robber," Henry said. "But he knows the combinations to all the safes. And it's possible he stole keys to each of the stores when he was in there."

"Hmm," Carter said, shifting in his seat. "Well, all these robberies have occurred during the night. Maybe when we're here tonight, we can keep an eye on things and make sure there isn't another robbery."

"That's exactly what we were thinking," Jessie said. "We could take turns watching. If Grandfather drives the van over, we could bring sleeping bags and some of us could sleep in the back of the van while the others watched the store."

"That's a good idea," Carter said. "If your grandfather doesn't mind. I could park my car in the alley behind the store, and a couple of us could watch the back door from there. The rest of you could watch the front from your grandfather's van."

"I'm sure he won't mind," Violet said. "He'd want us to catch the robber."

"It's all settled then," Carter said. "I'll meet you kids here at nine o'clock. First we'll put up the message for Queenie. Then we'll spend the rest of the night watching the drugstore."

"And if we're lucky, we'll catch a robber," Henry said.

* * * *

That night, Grandfather drove the children over to the mall at eight forty-five.

"What an interesting way to propose to a woman," Grandfather said.

"Isn't it?" Jessie said. "Do you think Queenie will like it?"

"I think she will," Grandfather said.

"Even more important, do you think she'll say yes?" Violet asked.

"I think she will," Grandfather said again. "She and Carter have been good friends for a long time."

Grandfather parked right in front of the

sign. It read: TRY A LATTE AT THE JAVA CAFÉ.

"Hmm. A latte sounds good," Grandfather said. "I think I'll try and get one before the Java Café closes. Would you kids like something, too?"

"We've got snacks," Henry said, glancing at the small cooler that sat at his feet. The cooler was filled with bottles of spring water. A bag of apples sat next to the cooler.

"We'll just wait here for Carter," Jessie said.

There were only a couple of cars in the parking lot. The Game Spot, Lake's Jewelry Store, and Bob's Drugstore had all closed at eight o'clock. The Java Café was the only store at Crossroads Mall that was still open.

The children watched as Grandfather went into the coffee shop and came back out with a tall paper cup a few minutes later. Chip Douglas had followed Grandfather to the door. Grandfather said something to Chip, and Chip smiled. Then

Grandfather left, and Chip locked the front door.

"Carter hasn't arrived yet?" Grandfather asked when he returned to the van.

"Not yet," Jessie said, checking her watch. It was five minutes past nine.

The lights went out in the Java Café, then Chip stepped outside. He double-checked that the door was locked, then walked across the parking lot to a small red sports car. He got in and drove away.

A few minutes later, Carter drove up in a silver sedan. He parked right beside the Aldens.

"Sorry I'm late," he said when he got out of his vehicle. "I was with Queenie and couldn't get away."

"That's okay," Violet said. "The Java Café just closed. We probably wouldn't have wanted to put the message up until everyone had left the mall, anyway."

"That's true," Carter said.

"Do you have all the letters?" Benny asked.

Carter patted the inside pocket of his

jacket. "Right here," he said.

So they all went over to the sign.

"First we'll have to pull all these letters off," Carter said. "I'll keep them and give them to George later. But right now I don't want any other letters interfering with my message."

The children helped Carter pull the message about the Java Café off the sign. Then they helped him put up the new message. When they finished, they stepped back to admire their work.

PLEASE MARRY ME QUEENIE POLK.

"That looks nice," Jessie said.

"It should be the first thing she sees when she pulls into the parking lot," Carter said.

They all went back to the two vehicles.

"So, what is the plan for the rest of the night?" Grandfather asked. "Would you like me to stay parked where I am?"

"Yes," Carter said. "I brought some walkie-talkies so we can stay in contact." He opened the front door to his car,

reached in and pulled out a walkie-talkie, then handed it to Grandfather.

"I'm going to drive around to the back," Carter went on. "Perhaps Henry and Benny can come with me. Jessie and Violet can stay with you, James. If you see anything suspicious, call me on the walkie-talkie. I'll do the same."

Jessie nodded. "Sounds like a plan."

Henry and Benny got into the back seat of Carter's car and Carter drove off. Jessie and Violet got comfortable in the back of the van. Then they waited.

About an hour after they'd arrived, Jessie saw a dark figure approach the drugstore.

CHAPTER 10

Setting a Trap

"Wake up, Violet," Jessie nudged her sister. "Grandfather, look!"

Someone was inserting a key into the front door of the drugstore. And the person was too short to be Bob, the store owner.

Grandfather picked up the walkie-talkie and said, "We've got someone entering the drugstore through the front door. Could be an employee, but given the late hour, I think we better go check it out."

The walkie-talkie crackled, then Carter's

voice came over it. "Copy that. We'll wait here in case the person tries to make a get-away through the back door."

Violet, Jessie, and Grandfather slipped quietly out of the van and tiptoed across the parking lot. The drugstore was still dark.

Jessie tried the door. It was unlocked. "Let's go in," she whispered to Violet.

Violet nodded as Jessie pushed the door all the way open.

"Hello?" Grandfather called. There was a panel of light switches beside the door. Grandfather flipped them all and light flooded the store.

Jessie and Violet squinted in the sudden brightness.

There was a rustle in the back of the store. Then footsteps. Someone was running out the back.

Jessie, Violet, and Grandfather followed the sound of the footsteps through the store, through the back room, and out the back door.

Tony Silver stood with his hands above

his head. Carter's headlights lit up the whole alley.

"The police are on their way," Carter said as he held up his cell phone. Henry and Benny stood on either side of him.

"How can you be the robber?" Benny asked, shielding his eyes from the bright headlights. "You sell safes. You're supposed to keep people's money safe."

"I know." Tony hung his head in shame. "But I've got a lot of credit card bills. I can't seem to get ahead. And breaking into these stores is just so easy. I know all the combinations to the safes because I help the store owners set them. And getting keys is easy, too. Everyone seems to leave spare keys lying around. I know it was wrong, but I just couldn't help myself."

"So you're the one who put CARTER ROBBER on the sign out front?" Carter asked angrily.

Tony nodded. "I saw you taking letters off that sign one night. And so did Bob. I thought people might believe you were the robber since a couple of people already knew you were sneaking around the mall late at night."

"I would never rob anyone," Carter said.

"No, I suppose you wouldn't," Tony said.

They all heard sirens in the distance. The sirens grew louder and louder as two police cars zoomed around the corner and pulled into the alley.

"This is Tony Silver," Grandfather told the officers when they got out of their vehicles. "We just caught him breaking into the drugstore."

A white-haired officer stepped forward and took out his handcuffs. "Tony Silver," he said, "you're under arrest."

* * * *

The Aldens didn't get much sleep that night. They wanted to be at the mall first thing the next morning so they could see Queenie's reaction to the sign.

Queenie smiled when she saw them. "What's all this?" she asked as she stepped out of her car. She hadn't noticed the sign yet.

"We just wanted to say good morning," Carter said cheerfully.

"And it is a good morning indeed," Queenie replied as they all walked across the parking lot. "I understand our robber was caught last night and I have all of you to thank for that."

"You were right about Raina all along, Queenie," Benny said. "She wasn't the robber."

"Of course she wasn't," Queenie said. "Raina can be a little bit scatter-brained, and she doesn't always make the best decisions when it comes to money. But she would never steal."

All of a sudden, Queenie stopped walking. Her bottom jaw dropped open and she looked at Carter.

"D-did you do this?" she asked, her eyes darting back and forth between Carter and the sign.

Carter took Queenie's hand, then got down on one knee right in the middle of the parking lot. With his other hand, he reached into his inside pocket and pulled out a small black velvet box.

"Oh, my goodness!" Queenie put her hand to her chest when Carter raised the lid of the box. A diamond ring gleamed in the sunlight.

"You'll make me the happiest man in the world if you say you'll be my wife, Queenie," Carter said.

"I-I don't know what to say," Queenie said shyly. Her cheeks were glowing. A smile played at the corners of her mouth.

"Say yes!" Benny blurted.

"Benny!" Jessie hissed. She put her finger to her lips.

But Queenie just laughed. "It's okay, Jessie. Benny's right. That's exactly what I should say." She turned to Carter, who was still down on one knee, and smiled. "Yes, dear. I'll marry you."

Carter took the ring out of the box and slipped it on Queenie's third finger. Then he stood up, and the two of them hugged.

The Aldens clapped and cheered.

A car that was trying to get past them honked.

"We better get out of the way," Carter said as the group moved quickly toward the sidewalk.

"We've got a lot of planning to do," Queenie said.

"I'm looking forward to it," Carter replied, smiling.

* * * *

On Saturday, the big Word Master tournament was held at the Game Spot. There was a children's tournament and an adult tournament. More than fifty people had signed up for both tournaments, which made the store unusually crowded.

Jessie had won all three of her games so far. So now she was seated at the yellow table in the Kids' Korner playing for the championship. A crowd of children had gathered around Jessie and her opponent, a serious-looking boy named Andy.

Andy was a little younger than Jessie, but

he was good at finding words. He was fast, too. Jessie knew she'd have to concentrate if she wanted to beat him.

While Jessie and Andy puzzled over the letters in round three, there was a sudden eruption of cheers from the front of the store.

Carter and a woman with straight blond hair stood up and shook hands.

"Congratulations, Carter," Queenie said as she presented Carter with a small trophy.

"Thank you," Carter said with a small smile.

Jessie turned back to the letters in front of her. She wondered how Andy was doing? Did he have more words than she did?

But she knew it was a mistake to worry so much about her opponent. It was better to simply look at the letters in front of her and do the best she could.

Finally, the game was over and they counted up their points.

"I have 212 points," Jessie announced. "How many do you have?"

"I have 204," Andy replied. He reached

across the table to shake Jessie's hand. "Good game."

"Good game," Jessie echoed. "Maybe we can play again sometime."

Andy nodded. "I'd like that."

Jessie and Andy started picking up the game. Queenie came over and handed Jessie a small trophy. Carter and Raina stood right behind Queenie and clapped. So did Grandfather, Henry, Violet, and Benny.

"Thank you," Jessie said with a grin. She turned the trophy around and looked at it. It had a gold cup on top of a wooden pedestal. The lettering on the front of the pedestal read WORD MASTER CHAMPION. It was identical to Carter's trophy.

"Perhaps the two Word Master champions should play a game next," Carter suggested, once everyone except the Aldens had left.

"Really?" Jessie asked eagerly. "You'd play a game with me, Carter?" He had said no when Jessie had asked him before.

"I'd be honored. In fact," Carter gestured for everyone else to come and sit down, "why don't we all play a game? Just for fun?"

"Don't mind if I do," Grandfather said as he pulled out a chair and sat down. The children, Queenie and Raina sat down, too.

Then Carter divided up the letters and they all got ready for another game.